The Assassins' First Date

The Assassins' First Date

~~~

J.A. Kazimer

CAMEL PRESS

Seattle, WA

CAMEL PRESS

Camel Press
PO Box 70515
Seattle, WA 98127

For more information go to: www.camelpress.com
www.jakazimer.com

This is a work of fiction. Names, characters, places, brands, media, and incidents are either the product of the author's imagination or are used fictitiously.

Cover design by Sabrina Sun

The Assassins' First Date
Copyright © 2016 by J.A. Kazimer

ISBN: 978-1-60381-327-3 (Trade Paper)
ISBN: 978-1-60381-328-0 (eBook)

Library of Congress Control Number: 2016934774
Printed in the United States of America

For my best puppy friends,

Bodie & Killer,

And to the love of my life,

Ralphe B.

Dear Reader:

I know you have plenty of entertainment options, so thank you so much for choosing this novella to enjoy in your free time. The story is close to my heart for many reasons, the main one being it's the start of the Assassins series.

If you've read *The Assassin's Heart*, you've met Ben and Six, witnessed their daring and their desire. In this prequel, you will feel their growing attraction and their longing for what could and maybe will be if both of them are willing to take the risk.

You will also meet Nate Taylor, the hero of the forthcoming *The Assassin's Kiss*, a man with an eccentric past, an ex-wife, and a mounting hunger for a woman who has his fate in her hands. *The Assassin's Kiss* is Nate's tale, in case you fall in love him as much as I did.

I hope you enjoy this novella and all the novels in the Assassins series as much as I enjoyed writing them.

With much appreciation and warmest regards,

—J.A. Kazimer

Chapter 1

~~~

HANNAH WINSLOW, BETTER KNOWN as Six to her friends and enemies alike, checked her watch for the third time in ten minutes. "He's late," she whispered to her empty apartment. As usual the room failed to respond. Normally that wouldn't bother Six. She liked being alone, liked relying on herself. But tonight, as she waited for the man's arrival, the cold silence was getting under her skin, lodging there like a splinter.

"Where the hell are you, Ben?" she asked after another five minutes passed. He'd been due to pick her up over thirty minutes ago for dinner at a swanky restaurant Six had been dying to try. She ran her hand down the sleek little black dress covering a good third of her body. It hugged her boyish curves in such a way that, for once, she looked like those girls in the rap videos. Her makeup was carefully applied, heavier than she liked—but sometimes you needed to hide behind layers of mascara. Her hair was part of the disguise; its natural russet color was currently dyed a bright blonde and cut short into a messy bob.

While Six liked the style, the color reminded her of the sun-bleached cheerleaders of her youth, those girls who'd never quite accepted the 'new girl.' In fact, Six had never fit in, no matter where she found herself.

Until she met Benjamin Miller.

They'd worked together for a little over two years now, spending many hours in each other's company, but tonight would be far different. Six checked her lipstick in the mirror hanging in the hallway next to her front door. A shiver ran up her spine—a jolt of anticipation, excitement, and a touch of fear. This was unknown territory.

Anything could happen.

If only Ben would show up ….

Six checked the clock on the wall again. Two more minutes had passed. Had something gone wrong? She shook her head. Ben always planned for every possibility. If he was late, he would have a damned good reason why. Or so she told herself, even though her stomach knotted more and more with each second the clock ticked.

When she was just about to scream, a knock sounded on her apartment door. Not one to play coy, Six ripped open the door and froze. Standing in the archway, Ben looked good enough to eat in a black Armani suit and indigo tie that matched both the color and dangerous glint in his eyes.

Ben looked equally perplexed by the woman in front of him. His smirk was at odds with the burning desire in his gaze. "You clean up nice," he said with a wolfish grin.

"Gee, thanks," she responded, slipping around him and

into the hallway. She locked her apartment door and then turned to Ben. "Our reservation was for seven thirty."

"They'll hold it." He followed her down the corridor. They reached the street without saying another word, each lost in thought. Ben opened the passenger door of a black BMW, motioning for Six to enter. She did, hiking her dress to mid-thigh. Ben's gaze locked on the rising fabric. Taking a shuddering breath, he sealed Six inside the vehicle and walked around the front of the car to the driver's side door. Taking a deep breath, he exhaled through his mouth. Once inside the sleek vehicle, he wrinkled his nose and asked, "New perfume?"

Six winced. That was the last time she spent good money on the latest trendy signature scent. From the pained look in Ben's eyes, she might as well have rolled around in a Dumpster. "Is it that noticeable?"

"I like it," he admitted.

"Oh." She paused, looking straight ahead. "Thanks."

"You're welcome." He started the engine and eased the car into traffic. He drove just like he did everything—with complete confidence and power, two of the qualities Six liked best about him. "Nervous?" he asked, dragging her from her thoughts.

She shook her head. "It's a simple dinner date. What's there to be nervous about?" Both of them knew it wasn't that simple. Nothing ever was. Not where Ben and Six were concerned. But Six wasn't about to show her hand. She pressed down on her stomach, hoping to ease the jumble of nervous energy.

"I talked to Paul before I picked you up," Ben said, referring to their boss. "He's not too happy about any of this."

Her eyebrows rose. "Is that so? I hope you told him where he could—"

Ever the diplomat, probably a result of being born to one, Ben said, "I laid everything out, and he eventually came around."

She snorted. She could only imagine how that conversation went. For being a corporate type, Paul wasn't a bad guy. Ben seemed to trust him. But Six wasn't sure. He played his cards close to his vest, so she never quite knew where he stood. She wouldn't let him destroy her shot at making things right tonight. No matter what. "Good. Now we can do what we do best."

Ben grinned. "Argue about who's on top?"

"Sadly you never win." She laughed. "Even with so much practice."

He shrugged, a smile on his lips. "I've heard practice makes perfect."

"If that was the case," she said with a smile, "you'd be a better shot by now." Much too soon, things would turn serious. Deadly serious. But for now, with the mild night air wafting through the car window and her partner at her side, things were as relaxed as they could be for those who made a living on the razor's edge.

As usual, Ben allowed her barb to roll off his back. Being the second best shot wasn't anything to sneeze at. Not when the best shot could hit a gnat at a thousand yards. As Ben often told her, "Thank God and the CIA for recruiting you at a young age. Who knows what kind of damage you could've done if you played for the other side?"

She wasn't sure if that were true. But today, at this moment, she felt like she was in the right place, making the world a safer place. She'd worked for OPS—a CIA shell corporation—for almost three years now. Sometimes she spent weeks in faraway deserts, wrapped in traditional garb as the sun seared her skin, waiting for a target to enter her sights. At other times, like tonight, she got to play dress-up in order to finish a job.

Tonight's target was unusually dangerous. A man who'd spent his life inflicting pain on others. An arms dealer with a taste for the sex trade. Too many women had suffered at his hands. Had died because of him. Six vowed that tonight this man would take his last breath.

Chapter 2

~~~

BEN WASN'T QUITE AS sure about tonight's end game. He hated these up close and personal missions. Hated putting Six so close to danger. He liked her far removed, looking at the target through her sniper scope while he did the dirty, hands-on work, though he knew better than anyone that she could more than take care of herself.

Even armed with that knowledge, he tried to swallow the lump that grew in his throat at the thought. Too much could go wrong in an op like this. He'd seen many men die already, watched as the life blood poured out of his previous partners. Losing another was out of the question. He'd lost five already. Six was his sixth. Hence the nickname.

For Ben it was easier to deal with a number than a person. The moment he started thinking of her as 'Hannah,' he became vulnerable. An enemy could use that against him. He wasn't about to give anyone that kind of power over him, and over his missions.

He liked Six well enough. She was a good partner. Someone he could rely on in a pinch. She didn't whine or complain, like his former male sidekicks. She kept it together even when the odds were stacked against them. But beyond that, she was his business partner.

Nothing more.

So why did his gaze keep returning to her shapely tanned legs? And why did he keep noticing the way her black dress hugged every curve, emphasizing the woman underneath? How was it that her scent seemed seared into his senses?

Stop it, he ordered his treacherous libido. Hell, it had been too long since he'd spent more than a couple of naked hours with a woman. That was the only reason he was responding to Six. Once they got tonight's job done, he'd take a few days off to regroup, to enjoy the company of an available woman.

His eyes slid sideways to his partner. She sat with her hands folded in her lap, looking as if she didn't have a care in the world. But Ben knew better. While neither would admit it, tonight's assassination wasn't a run-of-the-mill job. The target had survived multiple attempts on his life already. So far he'd also murdered at least three of their fellow OPS agents and was believed to be responsible for the disappearance of many more.

"Let's review the plan," he said quietly. "I've arranged for us to be seated two tables from the target. He always orders the same fifty-year-old Scotch, an unopened bottle. Benson," he said, referring to another OPS agent, "switched out the bottles earlier today. There's enough

Special K in it to take down a horse." Good thing, too, since Special K was a horse tranquilizer. If it didn't kill the target outright, it would make Ben and Six's job a piece of cake.

Unless Benson somehow managed to screw up—a very real possibility, knowing the agent in question. Ben blew out a harsh breath. If they didn't take out the target tonight, more people would suffer at his hands. The thought stiffened Ben's spine and steeled his resolve. Even if he had to forfeit his own life, the target would fall. Tonight.

He didn't share his thoughts with his partner. There wasn't any need. Six would feel the same. He knew it as well as she did. It was their sworn oath.

Their assassin's creed.

Chapter 3

～～

THE TEAM OF ASSASSINS arrived at the restaurant ten minutes late for their reservation. The hostess glared at Six when she gave their name, but her scowl quickly gave way to a girlish giggle when she caught sight of Ben.

"Right this way," she purred, eyes devouring Six's partner. Six followed the hostess, summoning all her willpower to avoid smacking the voluptuous blonde. So Ben looked great in a suit and tie, his jet-black hair slicked back; it didn't give the hostess the right to ogle him openly in front of what might've been his wife or steady girlfriend. Six had half a mind to write a nasty Yelp review. She laughed at the thought, capturing the attention of Ben as well as that of half the men in the restaurant. Ben's fists clenched in reaction as he stared down each and every man lusting over his partner.

When they arrived at the table, located two tables from their target, Ben pulled out Six's chair. Her back was to the target, which left her both vulnerable and annoyed. Her heated glare told her partner what she thought of his high-handed tactics. He smiled in return, earning an even darker look. Without giving her a chance to stop him, he snatched the knife and fork in front of her and placed them out of reach. "In case you're tempted," he said with a wink.

She rolled her eyes but didn't argue. After all, filet of Ben wasn't on the menu this evening. She snuck a glance over her shoulder at their actual target, surprised by how different he looked from the surveillance photos they had of him. In the photographs, taken through a long lens, he oozed evil. Most of the images were grainy, his face shrouded in shadows. But here, in the dim light of the fancy restaurant, he looked like any lawyer, banker, or politician packing Washington D.C. on any given night.

Hell, he looked less smarmy than the three of them put together.

Then she caught a glimpse of his eyes. Cold, winter steel. Flat. There was nothing behind his gaze. No emotion. A chill ran down her spine.

Ben seemed to notice, for he removed his jacket and placed it around her shoulders. At first she thought his gesture was strictly gentlemanly, until she felt the hard steel of a Ka-Bar close combat knife in the inside pocket. She shook her head. It appeared that her partner was more nervous about tonight's mission than he'd let on.

He sat down in the seat across from her. From his vantage point, no move the target made would go unnoticed. That was Ben's specialty. He never left anything to chance. Some might say his training in the military had honed his skills. And they wouldn't be wrong. But there was more to it, Six knew. Ben had a sixth sense when it came to a mission. He never made a wrong move. This uncanny ability had saved their hides more than once. So she let him take point, knowing that when it was time, he would let her know.

~~~

HAD BEN KNOWN OF Six's blind faith in him, he might've folded under the pressure. For he didn't think of himself as anything more than a solider with a mission. He did what he had to do to get the job done. Careful not to attract the target's attention, he drew the menu closer and acted as if it held his complete interest. When what truly held his attention was the slightest movement Six made, the way her dress slithered up and down her skin.

Cursing himself, he cast his gaze back on the target and the bottle of expensive brandy the waiter had placed on the table. The only indication of Ben's rage was the tightening of his fingers on the menu. Six seemed to notice, for she snuck another glance over her shoulder as if she was interested in the ritzy restaurant décor.

"Damn," she whispered.

"Why'd he switch his drink of choice?" Ben fiddled with the menu. "Why tonight?"

"You think he's on to us?"

He set the menu down, and like a lover, took her hands in his. He pulled her fingers to his lips to cover his words. "I don't know. But I can tell you this: I don't like it. Something's off."

The slightest shift could mean the difference between life and death for an assassin. Too many times over the years Ben had learned that lesson the hard way. Five dead partners. Five families' lives forever changed. He wouldn't make that mistake again. Too much was on the line.

"What do you want to do?" Six asked, her lips curving into a seductive smile. If anyone noticed the beautiful young couple, they would never suspect they were discussing murder. Instead they appeared to be two people deeply in love.

He caressed her hand with his thumb. "Colombia."

"No back exit," she reminded him, referring to the escape plan they'd used in that South American country. "How about Beijing?"

"In a cocktail dress?" He chuckled. "I'd pay to see that."

She gave an exaggerated eye roll. "Fine. What other brilliant ideas do you have?"

"What about Three Card Monte?" he said, referring to one of the oldest and most effective con games around. "You create a distraction, some wine gets spilled, and he heads to the john to clean up. I take him out in the stall. We meet in the parking lot."

"And the bodyguards?" She jutted her chin in the direction of the two hulking figures standing guard over their target. Neither man looked like typical muscle, bulging with gym-sculpted physiques and large-caliber weapons, which meant they were pros. And that meant trouble. Pros wouldn't let Six close enough to spill wine, let alone allow the target a trip to the bathroom by himself. "Besides," she added, "Three Card Monte calls for three of us. Unless you have an assassin in your pocket, it won't play."

"Benson is in a van parked down the block," Ben said with reluctance. "He could play the third part."

Six laughed. "I'd rather gargle with glass. It would be a

cleaner way to die."

"Point taken." Ben glanced around the room. "We're running out of options here."

She closed her eyes. "I can do a version of the badger. Draw him to a hotel, and then take him out … when he … is otherwise occupied."

"Are you mad?" he growled. "This isn't some tool in a suit. He's a cold-blooded killer responsible for the deaths of three agents. Good agents."

"Ben," she said quietly, "I can do this. You know me."

The very thought of what could happen if things went sideways for Six while alone with the target turned Ben's insides to ice. He didn't see another choice, but he'd be damned if they'd fly blind. "All right. But we need backup to take out the bodyguards first." He paused, swallowing hard. "And if anything—I mean, anything—seems off, you bail."

She nodded.

He gripped her hands tighter. "I need to hear the words."

"If anything happens, I'm out. I promise."

He knew better than to believe her for a second.

~

SIX HEADED FOR THE ladies' room to calm her racing heart as well as uncross the fingers behind her back. She would complete the mission. If she died in the process, so be it. But the target would fall too. Tonight.

She understood Ben's hesitation. He felt a misguided sense of responsibility for her safety and the safety of others. Losing five previous partners had shaped his worldview. However, she disagreed. The most obvious way to complete the mission was to take advantage of her wiles and her skills. She was good with a knife. Untouchable with a gun. And she could hold her own in hand-to-hand combat. The CIA had spent years training her body to act and react like a machine.

Sometimes she longed for more. For a life outside the sniper scope.

But it wasn't to be.

She'd made her choice.

Chapter 4

～～～

NATE TAYLOR GLANCED AT the woman lying in bed next to him, racking his brain to come up with her name. It started with a C. He was fairly sure. Or was it a T? The cell phone on his nightstand blipped to life, indicating an incoming text message. Careful not to wake the sleeping albeit nameless woman, Nate rolled to his feet, snatching the phone before it buzzed again.

He checked the screen. A message appeared from H, his handler at OPS. The message was short and to the point, per usual—296, his code name, and another string of numbers indicating a location followed by the name of his contact, Benjamin Miller. He'd worked with Miller and his partner a few times. Both were damned good assassins. They got the job done without a lot of fuss and muss. Nate appreciated their work ethic, and seeing as how Hannah Winslow, better known as Six, was far from hard on the eyes, he was more than willing to join their band for this evening's entertainment.

He stabbed at the small letters on his phone, typing out a message for H. Some might think it odd that Nate's closest relationship was with a faceless person on the other end of the phone line. A person he'd never met. Never talked to in real life. Just letters on a screen.

Of late he'd found himself wondering more about H. He knew H was female. Or at least he suspected as much. It was the way she'd asked about his welfare following a recent mission. He'd taken a shot to the torso—nothing life-threatening, but he'd been out of commission for two weeks. H had expressed concern, as much as a string of letters could, which led to the assumption that H was a female. Men, in Nate's experience, would've made crude jokes about his reduced capabilities. Only a woman would show compassion.

With the exception of his ex-wife … or rather current wife, considering he'd yet to sign the annulment papers. Why give her the satisfaction? She'd left him to go running home to her rich stepdaddy before the ink on the marriage license was dry. Not that he fully blamed her. Nate wasn't marriage material. He refused to settle into a normal life, a byproduct of a bizarre upbringing at the hands of his eccentric mother and a parade of 'uncles.'

Julia, his ex, had wanted to walk on the wild side.

Nate had wanted a taste of normal.

They'd both regretted their choices.

Sometimes, late at night, when he was on a mission in a godforsaken land, Nate wondered about what might have been. His fantasies never lasted long, for that sort of thing could and would get an assassin killed.

H messaged back with fresh orders. Shaking off his dark thoughts, Nate read the message and then returned to the woman he'd left lying in his bed. In the spot where he'd once slept, a three-legged German shepherd now lay snoring on his pillow. A dog who'd served at his side during the worst years of his life, in Afghanistan. The dog had lost his leg when an IED exploded while the two of them were trying to disarm it. Nate had yet to forgive himself for the explosion, though Archie didn't hold a grudge as long as Nate kept his dinner bowl filled and the toilet seat up.

Nate glanced at the woman in bed with the dog. Thankfully, she hadn't stirred. It was hard enough having to explain his abrupt departure, but trying to explain while getting her name wrong was bound to end poorly.

He shook his head at his treacherous dog. "*Bleib*," he ordered the dog, a command to stay in German. The dog didn't bother to open his eyes. "Archie, *bleib*," he said again. "And I better not find drool on my pillow."

Archie's tail wagged once then stilled.

Seconds later, he let out a loud snore as a dribble of saliva lolled from his tongue.

Chapter 5

Mario LaCena, also known as 'the target', took a sip of brandy from the snifter, rolling the liquor around his tongue. His gaze flickered over the uninteresting sheep seated around the restaurant, men and women who obeyed some moral code until they dropped dead. And for what? These sheep didn't understand the rush of living life on the edge, of watching as another person's life force faded from their eyes. Mario understood the joy in the suffering of others. Some considered such a man a psychopath. But Mario knew better. He was a god. His will be done. On Earth, as there was no heaven.

He pictured the young girl, no more than twelve years old, waiting in his hotel room. He would break her spirit and then her body. She would beg, cry, and plead, and in the end, she would submit. That was what he liked best. Her total submission. Witnessing her realization that she was his to do whatever he wished with.

Most of the time the girls didn't survive the night.

Ah, but when one of them did …. He smiled, licking the exquisite liquor from his lips. But first, he had business to take care of. He glanced over at the couple a few tables away.

~~~

BEN CAST HIS EYES quickly around the restaurant. Six knew he was searching for anything out of the ordinary. When he appeared satisfied that all was well—or as well as could be under the circumstances—he cleared his throat. "They called Taylor in," he said.

Six nodded, a small smile on her lips as she pictured the muscular, good-looking military-trained man who had joined OPS less than a year ago. They'd worked together a few times since and she trusted him as much as an assassin could trust. "Things are looking up," she said to her partner.

"You will not hit on our backup," he said. She rolled her eyes, which brought a smile to Ben's hard mouth. "I mean it, Six. Taylor is here to help us, not be treated like a piece of meat."

"You're hilarious," she said. "Keep talking like that and you'll wind up back in sexual harassment training. And we all know how much you got out of the last session." Ben had left the last OPS sexual harassment training seminar with the trainer. The two had spent the weekend exploring the male/female dynamic.

"Sometimes you have to take one for the team." As he spoke the words, the two assassins sobered. The idea of 'taking one for the team' was all too familiar to OPS agents. Too many lives had been lost already. Neither Ben nor Six wished for further bloodshed. But the possibility of death was ever present. It could happen during something as seemingly innocuous as dinner at a fancy restaurant or as the result of accidentally locking eyes with the man you were sent to kill.

Ben's phone buzzed in his pocket. He withdrew it and checked the caller ID. "Taylor's here." He rose, setting the linen napkin in his lap on top of his nearly untouched plate of food. "I'll be back in a few minutes."

Six nodded, watching as he headed for the door marked Men's. As she turned back, her eyes caught the gaze of the target. He lifted his snifter of brandy in her direction. A shiver ran down her spine, but she ignored the sudden onset of terror and lifted her lips into a flirtation grin.

This, she knew deep in her heart, *is the only way*. Through the soft fabric of her clingy dress, she fingered the weapon strapped to her thigh.

It was time.

Chapter 6

~~~

"Taylor," Ben nodded to his fellow assassin as they stood inside the dark wood-paneled men's room. Thankfully the air smelled of urinal cake and expensive aftershave instead of the already digested main course. "Thanks for coming."

Nate returned his nod. "What's the play?" He motioned to the restaurant beyond the doorway of the men's room. He knew the way Miller thought, knew his sense of duty and purpose. This wouldn't be a half-assed job. Miller would have weighed every option, keeping his team as safe as possible. Nate trusted Miller's intellect, if not his skills.

Ben paused before answering, "The target has two bodyguards. Mossad, by the look of them."

Nate nodded again. Mossad agents were hardcore. Men and women willing to kill and die for the job—just like the two assassins plotting to kill their client. Nate had identified the Mossad agents right off by the way they held themselves—backs ramrod straight, eyes cold and watchful. Taking them out wouldn't be easy.

He smiled in anticipation.

"I'll draw them off," Ben said. Nate's smile broadened. That was so like his fellow assassin. The guy always tried to protect his team. He would always be the first in. It was what made him great, but one day it would be his downfall.

Or the downfall of his partner, Six.

The way Ben watched her when she wasn't looking spoke volumes. He wondered if they were sleeping together. Probably not. Sleeping with his partner wasn't Ben's style. He focused too much on the job. A pity, in Nate's opinion. If Hannah were his partner ….

"Once they're clear, Six will take out the target," Ben was saying. Nate nodded. He didn't doubt Hannah's skills, not in the least. Neither did Ben, but Nate could hear the underlying stress in his co-worker's voice. This wasn't an easy target. Mario LeCena was a hell of a dangerous man. A stone-cold killer.

"Oh, and Nate," Ben said with a quick grin, "try not to get shot. Again," he said, referring to when Nate took a bullet a few months ago. "I hate having to fill out all that paperwork."

~~~

BEN TOOK A DEEP breath as he slipped through the men's room door and into the main restaurant. The rattling of plates and the clinking of glassware filled the air, as did the scent of fifty-dollar steaks and thousand-dollar Scotch. He maneuvered past waiters carrying trays laden with mouth-watering signature dishes.

A woman screamed, and a wine glass shattered on a nearby table. Ben froze, his eyes searching the restaurant. He shuddered. He couldn't pinpoint the problem. Not just yet. Not until his gaze fell on his partner, straddling the target in a roomful of terrified witnesses.

Chapter 7

~

A N HOUR LATER, SIX still couldn't believe what had
happened. Nor could Ben, if his wide-eyed gaze
was any indication. He stood next to her, both of them
watching in silence as a gurney wheeled the late, far-
from-great Mario LaCena from the restaurant. She only
imagined the Yelp reviews tonight's guests would give
after the cops locked the place down. The order had
come from the local D.C. cops. Standard procedure when
dealing with a suspicious death. And LaCena's death was
as suspicious as they got.

Hell, Six had witnessed the whole thing and she had no
clue as to what had caused LeCena to clutch his throat
and fall to the ground, his lips turning bright blue.

Or who had done him in.

Ben, apparently, didn't share her wonder. For her
partner had been sneaking suspicious glances at her ever
since he'd hauled her off LaCena's corpse less than sixty

minutes ago. Not that she blamed him. The whole thing was like something a mystery writer would make up.

The OPS team had gone in aiming to kill their target. Not only had they failed, but someone else had completed the task, forcing Six into the precarious situation of trying to save the intended victim's life.

So that she could later kill him herself.

"How did you know the victim?" A detective in a freshly pressed suit with a haircut straight out of a 1950s television cop show flipped his notebook open and waited for Six to answer.

She licked her lips, wringing her hands both for show and to produce tears by digging her nails into her skin. When none readily appeared, she pressed harder until her eyes welled up. "I didn't. Not really."

The cop frowned. He was either sizing her up for handcuffs or falling for her act. If Six had to guess, she would have suspected the latter. Men had a tendency to see women in one light, a weak light at that. The cop confirmed her suspicion when he reached into his coat pocket and handed her a crumpled tissue. "Some of the other diners thought you were familiar with the victim." He gazed down at his notebook. "They claim you and the victim exchanged heated words before he collapsed."

"We—"

Ben interrupted before Six could say more. "Detective," he began in an authoritative tone—the same tone he used when ordering at the drive-thru. Six knew Ben always got what he wanted from the terrified teens who took his order.

Ben's tone had the opposite effect on the detective. The cop's eyes grew frosty. A master at reading others, Ben backed off. He slumped his shoulders and affected an air of beta-male. "My fiancée …" he began, wrapping his arm around Six's waist and yanked her close, so close that Six could feel his backup weapon, a small, snub-nosed .25, holstered at his side digging into her hip. "My fiancée and I are celebrating our three-month anniversary. You can imagine how this whole ordeal has put a damper on our evening."

"Of course," the cop said, the coldness leaving his gaze, "but you can also imagine my position. Your," his pause spoke volumes about his opinion of their relationship status, "*fiancée* was the last person to speak to the victim before he expired."

"She tried to save him."

"The diners said as much."

Ben's forehead wrinkled. "But you don't believe them."

"Let's just say," his eyes were fixed on Six's face, "for a pro, taking a life can look a lot like saving one."

Six gasped, her hand clutching her throat. A mistake, she soon realized, as the wound she'd created by digging her nails into her hands to generate a few tears drew the detective's eye. Defensive wounds, he probably assumed, injuries created while the victim struggled for breath. She was going to get the electric chair.

Nope, scratch that. They didn't use 'Old Sparky' anymore.

She'd find herself strapped down on a table awaiting a dose of lethal chemicals, all because she'd stupidly overplayed her hand.

The detective reached for her arm. Rather than break his offending limb as she was tempted to do, she allowed him to pull her hand to his. "Hey, Dunbar," he said to one of the men on his team, "we got nail marks and some blood. I want photographs and DNA swabs ASAP."

Ben glanced down at her hand, and then into her eyes. One dark eyebrow rose in what to her looked a lot like a smirk.

Chapter 8

～

NATE STOOD A FEW feet away from his fellow assassins, weighing the need to get involved. As much as he wanted to be a part of the action, he suspected everyone would be better off if the three assassins didn't appear connected. His suspicion was confirmed by the lead detective and his apparent heart-on for Six—in a person of interest sort of way. From the way the cop stared at the cleavage bursting from her dress, he had it bad. *Best to keep your distance*, the little voice in Nate's head declared.

But he had never been good at listening to that annoying little voice. Which explained his marrying a woman like Julia Jensen Harding. He'd known better. From the first moment they'd met. But he'd gone and done it anyway.

He had plenty of scars to prove it.

He reached into the pocket of his suit jacket for the appropriate hardware, and then rushed forward with little forethought as he was prone to do. "Detective," he said loudly, "if I may …."

The cop's gaze shifted from Six's cleavage to Nate's face. "Who are you?"

"My name is," he paused, trying to remember what the credentials in his pocket stated, "Jonathan Applebee." Again he paused, this time for effect. Nate had an easy time slipping into any role. Hell, he'd been conning marks since he could talk. "Special Agent Jonathan Applebee." Reaching into his jacket, he pulled out the forged FBI badge and ID. The black leather case was cracked and appeared worn enough to be authentic, likely because Nate had lifted it from a real FBI agent a few months ago. An agent who wasn't nearly as special as he'd thought when he insulted the barmaid at Nate's favorite watering hole. The fight had been over in two punches; Nate had graciously allowed the agent to take the first.

At the title 'Special Agent,' the detective practically saluted. Ben had the opposite reaction. The corner of his mouth twitched. Nate ignored his fellow assassin's obvious amusement. "Your name, Detective?"

"Bonewell, Special Agent." He held out his hand. "My name is Richard Bonewell."

Now both of Ben's lips were quivering. Six stepped on his foot to keep him from laughing. Nate reacted much the same way. No man of any age could resist laughing at a name as unfortunate as Richard Bonewell. He stifled his mirth quickly enough and took the detective's outstretched hand. "Please to meet you, Detective Bonewell. Can we talk privately for a minute?"

Richard agreed, leaving Ben and Six in the care of a mess of crime scene technicians who photographed and swabbed Six. The two men dodged yellow police tape outside to the brightly lit street, where cop cars, CSI vans, and an ambulance with LaCena's body, headlights off, were parked. Nate took a breath of fresh air. "Richard," he paused, "may I call you Richard?" A part of Nate—the thirteen-year-old boy part of him—wanted the detective to say, 'my friends call me Dick,' but sadly it wasn't to be.

"Please," the cop said. "And I'll call you—"

"Jon," Nate returned, ever the friendly FBI agent. "Do you have a positive ID on the victim?"

The detective nodded. "Guy's name was Mario Duke LaCena. A dirtbag with a sheet longer than my list of ex-girlfriends." He waved at the two Mossad bodyguards surrounded by uniformed policemen. "Those are his bodyguards. They ain't saying anything. But we got surveillance video from inside the restaurant. Or we will, as soon as Judge Reynard signs the damned warrant." He snorted as he motioned to the restaurant where fifty eyewitnesses and possibly a killer other than Nate's fellow assassins waited. "That place has more cameras in it then you guys got on the White House."

Nate had doubts about that. If he wanted, his analyst H could pull up video of the President's john. *You'd be surprised how many dirty deals go down in the head.* Nate rubbed his chin, thinking. Now might be a good time to get a look at the surveillance footage. Before the cops got their paws on it. If Six had done the guy, Nate needed to know how damning the video was, so they could get on top of it. "You think that woman," Nate pointed to the window where Ben and Six were barely visible behind the frosted glass, "did this?"

Bonewell rubbed his chin, his shoulders rising into

what appeared to be an unconscious shrug. "She sure is a looker. My second ex had a body like that. 'Course she left me for another man. Rich guy like that one." He motioned to Ben. "Heard she took him for all he was worth. Gold-digging bitch."

Nate's experience with his ex-wife, Julia, was oddly similar. She'd left him on their wedding night. Last he heard she was dating some slick politician with his eye on the presidency. He shook off the righteous anger that burned in his chest whenever he thought of Julia. "A woman like that," he waved vaguely at Six, "has secrets for sure. But is she a killer?"

"That's the question," Bonewell replied. "The eyewitnesses swore the victim and the suspect argued shortly before he fell to the floor. Then again, witnesses claim she tried to save the guy. I'm not sure what to make of her. Other than something ain't right about those two."

Nate cocked his head. "How so?"

"She ain't wearing a ring." He rubbed his chin. "And he ain't a sucker. Watch that guy's eyes. They don't miss a thing. Man like that, he don't fall for no gold-digger."

Nate had to hand it to the guy. He wasn't as dumb as he looked. Behind the ridiculous name was a cagey detective. The assassins would have to be careful. But right now Nate needed some alone time. Or rather, almost alone time. Just him and his phone.

Chapter 9

~~

MALE AND FEMALE COPS in all shapes and sizes buzzed around the scene of the crime. They shuffled eyewitnesses to the back of the restaurant, refusing to let even the highest ranking officials leave. After all, vital evidence could be lost.

And a killer might go free.

Crime scene techs bagged anything and everything, including the glassware from the table Ben and Six had shared. The very real possibility of fingerprint analysis of the stemware didn't bother Ben. As with all the OPS assassins, Ben's and Six's fingerprints were regularly wiped from federal, state, and local databases.

DNA profiles were another story. Touch DNA, a relatively new field of criminal investigations, was far more likely to link suspect DNA to a variety of crimes and crime scenes. It was impossible not to leave some impression at any scene, let alone a crime scene. Investigators were getting much better at DNA technologies. One day soon, it would be impossible to get away with murder.

Ben welcomed the challenge.

But not tonight. Tonight linking Six's DNA to the scene would destroy everything. He had one choice: he would have to taint the sample. Chain of evidence meant everything in a case like this; disturb it, and the evidence meant nothing. Nonetheless that would be a last resort.

First he had to get his partner alone and find out why she'd performed CPR on the very guy she'd been assigned to kill in the first place. Easier said than done, considering that the cops had separated the two assassins, keeping Six on the other side of the long wooden bar.

His chance came a few minutes later when Six excused herself to go to the ladies' room. Her eyes caught his in silent communication.

Ben waited a few minutes, pretending to check the highlights of the Capitals game playing on the muted television above the bar. Finally, he rose from the barstool where the cops had ordered him to sit. "I'm hitting the head. Got a problem with that?" he asked the young rookie, who looked too young to buy beer, let alone arrest someone.

The kiddie cop frowned but let Ben pass.

No wonder crime had spiked in the district, Ben thought, wanting to smack the kiddie cop in the back of the head. If the kid stayed that trusting, he'd be lucky to survive the year.

With a sigh, Ben headed to the john. After first making sure no one was paying attention, he slipped through the door marked *Ladies*. Six waited on the other side, her face intent. Ben frowned at the faint bruises on her arm—

bruises that hadn't been there two hours ago. "Only you could kill a man and then give him mouth-to-mouth."

Six smiled. "Not quite."

His eyebrow rose.

"I didn't give him mouth-to-mouth."

"I see."

She laughed at his dry tone. "Since we don't have much time, I'll give you the Cliff's Notes version."

"I'm weak with anticipation," he joked, knowing humor made bad memories a little more palatable. Whatever Six had gone through in the minutes she was with LaCena hadn't been good. Why else would she have killed him in a roomful of people?

She rolled her eyes. "As soon as you went to meet Taylor, I made my move. I planned on enticing him away, but I quickly realized my mistake."

His eyes roamed up and down her body, noting the curves and the way the light reflected off her skin. His mouth went dry. "Gay?"

"Not that I could tell."

"So what was his deal?"

Her face hardened. "Us."

Chapter 10

~

SIX WATCHED BEN'S FACE as her words sank in. A parade of emotions crossed his features—though, to an outsider, he looked the same as he had a minute ago. But she had worked with him long enough to read each slight movement, like the involuntary tightening of his jaw or the way his gaze darkened.

The meaning of that single word was almost too much to fathom. "Our conversation started out pleasantly enough. He ordered us a round of drinks, a Cabernet circa 1920 for me and a brandy that cost as much as two months of my rent for him." Her lips curled with disgust. "FYI, the wine tasted like rubbing alcohol. Expensive rubbing alcohol but still unpleasant."

He grinned. "The perils of the lifestyles of the rich and infamous."

"He called me by my name," she whispered. "He knew my name, Ben."

"So there's a leak." His voice was as hard as steel. "He knew we were coming."

"Yes."

He lowered his eyes to the bruises on her arms. "I take it this is when the heated exchange occurred."

"Apparently Mario took offense at us trying to kill him." Mouth quirking into a grin, she shrugged her slender shoulders. "I tried to explain that he was a disgusting pig, but that made him take even greater offense." She held out her arm. "We wrestled a little, and then I knocked his hands away. The bodyguards leapt forward …."

"And?"

"LaCena collapsed to his knees, grabbing at his throat. I thought he was choking on something at first." She tried to hide a shudder of revulsion but failed. She hoped Ben hadn't noticed. Like all the male assassins in her acquaintance, he would probably take her reaction as a sign of weakness. She licked her lips. "I wasn't wrong. It was his tongue."

"It wasn't you who poisoned him?" he asked with what seemed like some measure of surprise.

She tried not to take offense. Ben knew her better than that. She would never leave a room full of witnesses. "We needed him alive in order to find out who sold us out."

"Hence the CPR."

"Yes." She wanted to stop her story there, for what happened next wasn't one of her finer moments. "But first I tried to get a name."

His smile was genuine then. "And did Mario share his juicy secret?"

"No," she said, annoyed. "If I'm ever murdered," a possibility they both knew was more than likely, "I plan to spill everything I've ever been told. Like the fact Kim Connors stuffed her bra in sixth grade."

"I'll make sure I'm there to hear every word."

"I thought you might," she said with a smile that quickly turned serious. "What's the plan now?"

"We find the leak," his smile grew deadly, "and we plug it."

~~~

NATE DUCKED UNDER A nearby awning to avoid the cold rain drizzling down. He'd ditched Dick a few minutes ago, saying something about FBI business. Dick hardly noticed; he had other things on his mind, namely fifty angry customers who had missed their main course.

Nate drew his smartphone from his pocket and quickly typed in his security cipher, followed by his code, 296. A few seconds later a text message popped up.

H: *Encrypted?*

296: Yes

H: *Go*

296: Need video

H: *10-20*

The code 10-20 was H's way of requesting the location of the video feed. Nate turned on his phone's GPS so H could track it. Less than thirty seconds later, a grainy black and white video feed appeared on his screen. He watched, mesmerized by Six's brief scuffle and later attempt at CPR on the very man she'd been contracted to kill.

Other than her perhaps-over-the-top efforts to save a man who was blue and foaming at the mouth, Nate didn't see anything Dick might find incriminating. Unless he dug deep enough to find out Hannah Winslow's true identity.

Nate's screen flashed with an incoming text.

H: *Get what you need?*

296: Yes

H: *PL update*

Shit. PL stood for his boss, Parker Langdon. The man had an uncanny ability to sense when it was time to cover his own ass. Other than that, and the fact he dressed and acted like a corporate tool, he wasn't too bad to work for. Nate's paycheck had never bounced. Still, Nate had a bad feeling about his continued employment and this particular mission. The less Parker knew, the better, at least until the assassins were clear.

H: *?*

296: Stall

H: *You owe me*

296: 10-4

Nate turned off his GPS and shoved his phone back in his pocket. He had to warn Miller about Parker's interest before it was too late.

Chapter 11

~~~

ABOUT AN HOUR LATER, Six stood in front of Detective Bonewell, sizing the man up. He looked like a typical TV detective, rumpled suit and shaggy brown hair badly in need of a trim. Divorced, she'd bet. The mustard stain on his tie was a good indicator. All in all, he didn't appear to be much of a threat. But Six knew better than to judge a man by his appearance. The best assassins were able to blend in, to assume the façade needed to get the job done. Maybe the good detective had watched too many reruns of *Columbo* and decided that persona worked for him.

Assumed façade or not, the man might prove dangerous. But first he'd have to stop staring at her chest long enough to finish his interrogation. His eyes roamed her body until she felt the need for a long, hot shower. She wasn't sure if he was sizing her up for a jail jumpsuit or planning her seduction. Either way, she was in serious trouble. "Tell me again what you and the victim talked about?" he said, his gaze settling once more on her cleavage.

"Hasn't she been over this enough?" Ben asked from his seat at the bar. He stood, looking much like an avenging angel of the dark variety as he swooped down to save her from the detective's evil clutches. *I need a drink*, she thought. *Before my imagination takes full flight.*

The detective tore his gaze away from Six to focus on Ben. "I will say when enough is enough. In case you've forgotten, a man is dead, and your," he paused as if to let them know exactly how little he believed in their so-called engagement, "*fiancée* was at his side when he died."

Ben took a step forward.

The detective's hand slid to the gun holstered at his side.

"We really didn't talk about anything," Six broke in, fearing that bloodshed might commence at any moment. "Darius went to the men's room," she said, using Ben's undercover name—one of many. "And the man … the one who died … he motioned me over for a drink. I accepted, and he ordered us a round. The drinks arrived. We toasted. And that was that."

"Is that so?" Bonewell said in a tone that conveyed his disbelief. "Care to explain the part of the video where you and Mr. LaCena get into a physical altercation?"

Tears filled her eyes. They were fake, but looked real enough to bolster her lie without her having to inflict further injury on her hands. "Mr. LaCena tried to kiss me. I shoved him away, and we struggled for a moment. He quickly apologized, blamed his actions on the brandy, and then he grabbed his throat and fell to his knees." At least that part was semi-true. She let out a sob. "I was so scared—"

"That you then straddled the victim, forcing his face

to yours." The detective paused. "And from what we can see on the video, LaCena appears to say his final words. Words that cause you to slap him in the face."

Six winced. In hindsight, she couldn't justify hitting a man who was struggling for every breath. As much as she wanted to defend her actions with a 'he deserved it' declaration, she kept her mouth shut. She doubted that true statement would keep her out of lockup.

Nate cleared his throat, loud enough to get the threesome's attention. "Detective, to me, it appears as if Ms.," he motioned to Six, snapping his fingers as if trying to remember her name, "Barber was rendering aid."

"Yes," she declared. "Mr. LaCena was slipping away. I slapped him to keep him with us."

The detective seemed to buy her answer, for he moved on. Sort of. "And his final words, Ms. Barber? Did he name his killer?"

Good question. Six wondered the same. Mario LaCena's last utterance started with the letter R. That's all she'd been able to make out. When the detective pressed her further, she simply shook her head. "No," she said.

"Are you sure?" he asked almost too earnestly, as if his job, if not his life, depended on it. She had a feeling it might. A detective who let a killer get away in a restaurant filled with very rich, important politicians wouldn't be a detective long.

Shaking her head slowly, she motioned to the spot where LeCena had said his last words. "If he knew his killer, he took the name to his grave."

Chapter 12

～

"He's not buying your innocent act," Nate said a few minutes later as the three assassins gathered in the large industrial cooler. Nate had scoped the kitchen out earlier, deciding the cooler offered the best meeting space to avoid prying eyes, ears, or whatever other body parts were interested in their conversation. From the way Hannah kept her arms crossed tightly over her chest, she didn't appreciate his location choice.

Hannah shot him a frown. "I *am* innocent, Taylor. Mario LaCena hit the floor before I could perpetrate any violent acts." Both men raised their eyebrows. "Fine, before I could perpetrate any murderous acts."

"In other words, she didn't do it." Ben grinned. "Case closed."

"If only," Nate responded, dampening the mood. "Bonewell, and I mean this in the nicest way, has a boner for Hannah."

For a second Miller looked blank at the use of Six's God-given name. "I told her not to show so much leg. It's distracting."

Even if Hannah didn't, Nate saw right through Ben Miller's statement. Sure, a nice set of legs grabbed a man's attention, but the fascination ended as soon as he realized there was no possibility said legs would ever be wrapped around his neck. Apparently Miller still harbored some hope.

Six rolled her eyes. "Hah-hah. Can we move this along before my trigger finger gets frostbite?" A dangerous possibility when one lived by the gun. "Barney Fife out there isn't going to arrest me."

"Is that so?" Nate said. "Because I have the distinct feeling you'll end up in handcuffs before the hour is out." All three assassins understood the danger of arrest. Booking photos. Fingerprinting. And worst of all—okay, second worst when one considered the stainless steel toilets—was the now standard DNA swab. The one and only thing bound to unmask an assassin. And once an assassin was burned, all bets were off. Enemies crawled from the woodwork like the cockroaches they were.

Ben rubbed his chin. "So we have one option."

Hannah nodded, and Nate followed suit. It wouldn't be easy.

But it had to be done.

The three killers had to find out who had murdered their target.

Before they could.

The very idea left a bad taste in Nate's mouth.

~

NATE'S CELL PHONE BUZZED from inside his pocket. He freed it, glancing at the incoming text. "I have to take this," he said to his fellow assassins and slipped out the cooler door. Ben and Six watched him leave. The only sound inside the freezer was the hum of the electronics.

Ben broke the silence first. "Whoever took LaCena out had to be working for someone else. Someone who knows about us ... about OPS."

While Ben felt bad about keeping the information from Nate, he was right when he said the less Nate knew, the better. Not that they didn't trust him. They did. With their lives. But not with this. Not when the truth had such wide-reaching ramifications.

And the truth was ... Mario LaCena was killed because he was a danger.

To someone close to them.

Someone who knew fully of Ben's original plan.

Someone who'd warned LaCena.

And as far as Ben knew only three people had that information.

Himself. His partner.

And the man who gave the order to kill LeCena in the first place.

Parker Langdon.

The Director of OPS.

Chapter 13

~~

"WHY WOULD LANGDON ORDER us to kill LeCena and then tip the target off to the plan?" Six asked, biting her lower lip.

Ben dragged his eyes away from her mouth. "Who knows? But I plan to find out."

The sound of heavy boots on the kitchen tile outside the cooler reached her ears. She held up her hand for quiet. After a few minutes the thudding receded. The cops were looking for her. She could feel it. "We can deal with Parker later," she said when Ben stayed quiet. "But right now, to keep me out of jail, we need to provide another suspect to the good detective." She pulled at the hem of her dress. She swore that the cold air had shrunk the material. The damned dress had a mind of its own as it revealed more and more leg. Good thing her partner didn't notice her distress. It was embarrassing enough to have her nipples as hard as pebbles when discussing the possibility that they worked for a madman, but if her dress shrunk any further, Ben would see far more than Paris, France or her underpants. "On a silver platter, because Bonewell doesn't strike me as the deep-thinking type."

Ben grinned, his expression losing its hard edge as his gaze fell on the rising hem of her dress. "Don't let the name fool you."

"Right," she said with a grin. "I think it was Plato who said—"

"Smartass." He chuckled. "Okay, so let's think this through."

"Whoever killed LeCena had to put the poison in the last round of brandy." Without her asking, Ben pulled off his jacket and tossed it at her. She put it on without comment, thankful it hung to her thighs, which was much more than her magically shrinking dress did. "We need to 'speak' to the waiter who served it," he said. "He's our prime suspect."

"Should be easy enough," she said with a quick grin of anticipation.

~~~

THIRTY MINUTES LATER, THE team decided 'easy' wasn't exactly the word they'd use to describe their meeting with the waiter. It started out well enough. Nate flashed his fake badge and brought the man to the kitchen, saying he had a few questions to ask him. The waiter, a man in his early thirties with curly brown hair, agreed without hesitation. In fact he looked eager to help.

Until he saw Ben waiting outside the cooler.

The waiter stopped dead in his tracks, and he turned to Nate. "What is this?" he asked, his voice trembling.

Nate gave him what he thought was a reassuring smile. The man flinched. Using his size, Nate pressured the man forward. Ben opened the cooler, and again the waiter balked. "Take it easy," Nate said. "We only want to talk."

"I … didn't … d-do … anything," he stammered.

"It's okay," Nate repeated, shoving the waiter into the cooler. At that moment all hell broke loose. The waiter launched himself at Nate, going for his eyes. Nate smacked the man in his jaw, and the waiter fell back. But he wasn't finished. He kicked out, catching Nate in the solar plexus. Nate grabbed his stomach, the air leaving his lungs with a whoosh.

Ben stepped toward him, grabbing the waiter around the throat. "Stop fighting. We just want to talk."

The waiter kept struggling.

Ben increased the pressure of his forearm against his windpipe.

The waiter tried to kick himself free, narrowly missing Ben's knee.

"A little help?" Ben said to his partner, who stood out of harm's way, wrapped in his jacket. She rubbed her chin as if debating. "Looks like you're doing fine on your own. Besides, I don't want to break a nail." She glanced down at her long, polished nails.

Nate finally recovered his breath. He punched the waiter in the jaw again, and the man slumped to the ground. Ben let him fall.

Nate quickly closed the cooler door. "Son of a bitch," he said.

Ben grinned. "Let's get him up and find out what he knows."

The two male assassins each grabbed an arm, lifting the

waiter from his slumped state. The man moaned, his eyes fluttering as he regained consciousness. "Please," he said, "I'll give you whatever you want."

"We aren't going to hurt you," Six said, glaring at the assassins holding him. Nate had to laugh. Hannah sounded like a schoolteacher negotiating with a rebellious student. "We just want to ask you a few questions."

The waiter nodded.

"Good." She gave him a soft smile. "Let's start with your name."

"George."

"Okay, George," she said. "Can you tell me what happened tonight?"

The man's face fell. "I knew it. I should've never trusted that guy. But he swore it was a prank, that nothing bad would happen."

This was good, Nate thought. They had a lead. A man. "What did this man say exactly?"

"He came into the restaurant around five. He told me his friend had a reservation for eight. Said it was his friend's birthday and he wanted to prank him." George paused, licking his lips. "He gave me a hundred dollar bill."

"To do what?" Six asked. "What did he want you to do?"

The assassins released his arms, and George dropped to the floor. Tears ran down his cheeks. "I thought it was a joke—"

"What did you do?" Six yelled.

Nate winced as George's face grew even paler. "Easy," he said to Six, who looked ready to add a few more bruises to the waiter. "George," he said in his most reassuring tone, "this is important. A man is dead." A man who deserved to die, but George didn't need to know that. "Tell us what you did after the man gave you the money."

George looked up, falling for the good cop/bad cop routine. Assassins 101. "I …. He gave me a bottle of booze. I was to replace it with the top shelf bottle in the bar." He started to cry loudly now. Nate grew more disgusted. "Was this man about five foot ten and balding?"

George sobbed a yes. "He looked like an extra from *The Sopranos*."

Damn. Nate turned to Ben. "Benson."

"Sounds like it." The man who'd paid George was an OPS agent who'd apparently screwed up his mission in the first place. He was supposed to have placed a Special K-laced bottle of Scotch on the shelf early that morning before anyone arrived at the restaurant. So why had he given the waiter a poisoned bottle of brandy this afternoon?

Ben reached for his phone to find out why he hadn't followed the plan, but George's next words stilled his hand. "Twenty minutes before Mr. LaCena arrived, he came back."

"What?" Ben growled.

George shrank into himself. "He gave me another hundred and took the bottle back."

"The bottle of brandy?"

The waiter shook his head. "No, it was Scotch. An expensive bottle too."

Chapter 14

~~

"So Benson took our bottle," Six said. "Why?"

Ben frowned. Although he didn't have a ready answer, he sure as hell planned to find out. But more importantly, they still had no clue as to who killed LaCena or how they'd done it. The brandy seemed like the most obvious murder weapon. But the cops had already bagged and tagged the bottle as evidence. Normally Ben would dial up an analyst at OPS to pull the test results from the local cops, but the more distance they kept from their employer at the moment, the better.

He said as much to his fellow assassins.

Six agreed, but Nate hesitated. "I think H can help."

"Can or will?" Ben asked. He was old school. He did his own recon, never asking for or trusting the info the faceless, nameless analysts gave unless he could see, feel, or taste it for himself. "You trust H?"

"With my life." He paused. "More than once."

"Okay then," Ben replied. "We need the tox results and fast."

"On it," Nate said, taking his phone from his pocket. "And what will you do while I'm doing all the work?"

Ben grinned. "Six is going to distract the detective while I get a look at the physical evidence they've collected so far."

～

"GOLD-DIGGING TRAMP," BEN YELLED at Six, or rather Kendra Barber, as the fake driver's license in her purse read. "How dare you cheat on me!"

Six made a grab for Ben's arm, missed, and dropped to her knees. "Please baby … it's not like that. I love you." The plea in her voice reached the farthest diners, who for the last two hours had been starved for entertainment while the cops photographed every bit of evidence. As much as Six hated weak women willing to beg for crumbs of affection from a man, she did rather enjoy her and Ben's well-crafted performance. Their present ploy was meant to give Ben a reason to storm out so he could get a look at the evidence in the CSI van parked outside and provide a setup that would allow Six to take advantage of Detective Bonewell's interest in her.

At first Six had balked, seeing no reason for getting any closer to the detective than she had to. If it came down to her arrest, she would find a way to free herself before the cops took her DNA. She was well versed in hand-to-hand combat and wielding weapons of all kinds, so the cops would certainly walk away bloody.

And Six would just walk away.

Ben had quickly nixed her plan. While in most

circumstances they were equal partners, Ben was technically her superior. That fact didn't bother her as much as it should. He rarely pulled rank on her, unless he felt her life might be in danger.

Then Ben acted like a mother hen.

Sometimes she wondered if his over-protectiveness stemmed from a desire to avoid a mound of paperwork and having to break in partner number seven. But sanity always prevailed: Benjamin Miller was a soldier.

He cared about one thing and one thing only—completing the mission.

And right now, her part in that mission was to slap Ben across the face as he called her a worthless tramp. A slap she enjoyed more than she should. Before she could slap again, Ben grabbed her arm and threw her backward, right into the arms of the detective. All according to plan.

He stormed out of the restaurant.

Not one of the cops followed.

Six smiled, rubbing her stinging hand.

Chapter 15

~~~~

A CHILL RAN UP Nate's spine, a chill that had nothing to do with being locked in a cooler with a waiter named George. A waiter currently tied up and gagged with Nate's tie. His favorite tie. He'd nearly said as much to Miller when the assassin had requested the item. Thankfully he'd kept his mouth shut. Ben didn't seem to be in the joking mood right now. Not with the very real possibility that OPS had double-crossed the assassins, leaving them hanging out to dry.

In his last exchange with H, the analyst had warned Nate that their boss, Parker Langdon, was paying special attention to the status of the investigation surrounding the assassination attempt and the murder of LaCena. There were only two reasons for this concern to Nate's way of thinking. Either Parker was finally taking an interest in his ops, or—far more likely—he had an iron in this particular fire. Until Nate knew more, he thought it best to avoid Parker.

Lucky for him, H was willing to forgo the normal channels and provide Nate with the information he needed—namely, the preliminary autopsy report and the tox screen of the brandy bottle.

While he waited for H to get back with the reports and his partners to stage their little play, Nate decided to casually interrogate the restaurant staff. Minus George, there were fifteen waiters on staff, three bartenders, and a hostess. Most claimed not to have seen anything suspicious—other than Six and the victim's altercation—before or after LaCena's death.

Nate mapped out each of the staffers' positions at the time of the murder. The third bartender, a woman named Jill, intrigued Nate the most. She'd poured the questionable brandy, and that made her a suspect in Nate's mind. "The brandy you served the victim. Where did it come from?"

Her pale face grew even whiter. "The owner's private stock. He okays us using it when a whale dines with us."

"And LaCena was a whale?"

She nodded. "He comes to the restaurant every month, on the first Saturday at eight, like clockwork. He always orders the same thing, a Dalmore Single Malt, 1939, and a Wagyu steak, rare. Except for tonight. Tonight he wanted a brandy."

Nate quickly did the math. "Easily a three-thousand-dollar ticket. How'd he pay for it?"

"He didn't."

An alarm sounded in Nate's head. "Who did?"

Jill looked right and then left as if afraid to be overheard.

"The government, is my guess. I think he was some kind of spy or something."

~

NATE HAD JUST FINISHED up with the staff when his smartphone buzzed to life. He checked the message and frowned. H had come through. Somehow she'd managed to get both the preliminary autopsy results as well as the toxicology report on the brandy. When Nate finished the second read-through of the reports, he closed his eyes and swore softly.

Chapter 16

~~

BEN'S TRIP TO THE evidence van lasted less than two minutes. Ten seconds was all it took to pull on a pair of gloves and pick the lock. He quickly checked the evidence log, finding LeCena's cell phone. He scanned his incoming and outgoing call list. Not a single number popped up. Either LeCena hadn't made a single phone call, or someone had wiped the data. Ben's blood froze at the possibility. This killer wasn't some run-of-the-mill hit man for hire. They were dealing with a serious pro.

Flipping through the evidence log again, he found the place settings and silverware from his and Six's table and hauled them out of the bagged evidence pile. He wiped the prints off the silverware and glasses before placing it all back in the stack. Next he lifted the blood and fingernail swabs the evidence techs had collected from Six. He took the small bottle of sanitizer—it was much like the kind used to kill bacteria, but in this case it killed

DNA—from his pocket, dousing each swab. The brandy bottle was his last task. He hefted it from the mound and stuffed it under his jacket. He would stash it in the alley for safekeeping.

That should do it, he thought with a grin as he stepped from the CSI van unnoticed.

~

"ARE YOU ALL RIGHT?" the detective asked Six, his eyes for once on her face. She bowed her head, both to keep him from studying her features and to give him a feeling of superiority—something few men could resist.

Ben was one of them.

"I … ah …." She let out a soft sob, running her fingers down the detective's chest. Her disgust level rose with each hairy inch. "Do you think he'll forgive me?"

The detective didn't answer.

But his erection spoke volumes.

She wasn't sure she could keep his attention for long. Not without needing a very hot shower.

With her body pressed against his, making her aware of the outline of both his erection and the weapon fastened to his side, Six could only think of one option. She faked a dead faint.

I definitely didn't think this through, she thought just before her head hit the floor. The damned detective failed to stop her descent.

She landed hard, cursing men in general and Ben in particular.

~

BEN'S GOOD HUMOR OVER his successful search of the evidence van didn't last long.

Back inside the restaurant cooler, he shook his head, unable to believe the autopsy report Nate showed him. "The brandy didn't kill him."

"He wasn't poisoned?" Six asked, shock in her tone.

"No," he responded, "he was poisoned. Just not by the brandy."

"You're kidding me." She started to pace, the hem of her dress rising as she moved. Ben couldn't help it. His gaze fell to her toned upper thighs, and suddenly he pictured those thighs wrapped around his waist. *Thank God for the cooler*, he thought. Sporting a serious bulge while reading an autopsy report would be difficult to live down.

With great effort, he tore his eyes away from the tempting sight and focused on Nate. He frowned when he noticed Nate eyeing Six's legs too. Red hot jealousy burned in Ben, a new and unwelcome feeling. Benjamin Miller didn't get jealous. He was a love 'em and leave 'em sort of guy. One bad marriage and an even worse divorce was more than enough. He was being ridiculous. Six was his partner. That was it. He didn't and wouldn't think of her in that way again. She deserved his respect.

But my God, she was killing him with that dress. The hem had risen even higher, revealing a black lace garter belt.

And a Seecamp LWS .32 pistol.

"Stop," Ben said, breathless as if he'd run a mile. "Please, Six, you're making me dizzy with all that pacing. We need to think."

"Here's what we know," she said, pausing mid-step. "LaCena regularly comes here. His bill is comped by some government agency. OPS wants him taken out. We devise a pretty damn good plan, which goes to hell when Benson either fucks up or is ordered to retrieve the poisoned Scotch."

"Knowing Benson, I'm guessing he had orders from higher up." Ben rubbed his chin. "He's not the kind of guy who thinks for himself. Then there's Parker. I briefed him on the plan yesterday and he didn't seem at all interested. Barely paid attention."

"According to H, Parker's now monitoring our situation closely." Nate frowned as he checked his phone. "The bastard clamped down on any communications. H has gone dark."

Damn, Ben thought. Nate's analyst had been a great help so far. Without her, the odds of finding the killer dwindled. "What if OPS was the one paying the restaurant bill?" he asked, warming to his theory. "LaCena is Parker's informant. Maybe he threatens to walk, and Parker arranges a little show to keep him in line."

"Somehow he gets word to LaCena about us, about the assassination attempt," Six said. "That's why LaCena switched to brandy; he knew the Scotch was poisoned, or at least we all thought it was."

"Think about this," Nate jumped in. "What if someone found out LaCena was a rat, tattling to Parker, and they killed him to keep him from exposing them?"

"Or they hired someone to do it," Six said. "This was a professional hit."

Ben closed his eyes. "And only one assassin fits the profile."

"The Reaper," all three assassins said at once.

Chapter 17

~~~

IN THE MANY YEARS Ben had worked for OPS, he'd heard stories about the infamous killer known only as the Reaper. Not that he'd thought they were anything but tall tales. Until tonight. The man behind the legend had never been caught. Not a single photo taken. No one knew what he looked like. Even more impressive, not a single piece of evidence—fingerprint or tiny drop of DNA—had ever been collected against him. He simply slipped in, took out the target, and left, completely undetected. He was a ghost.

But not for much longer.

Ben would find him. And when he did, he wouldn't hesitate to kill him.

To do that, he needed to know exactly how LeCena had died. The autopsy report officially declared his death a homicide by an as-of-yet unknown substance. The toxicology report could take weeks to complete, considering the vast array of deadly poisons available, not to mention the staff cutbacks that meant everyone had to wait for results. According to Six, who had been up close and too personal with LaCena when he died, he presented all the typical symptoms of neurotoxic paralysis. His lips had quickly turned blue, a sure sign of respiratory failure.

The lab might dither over identifying the neurotoxin or blend of toxins, but Ben was in a hurry. It was Ben's new mission—that and stopping the Reaper permanently.

~

Six was not as optimistic as Ben about nabbing the Reaper. Even if they did discover exactly how LaCena died, the Reaper was likely a hundred miles away already, counting his stash of cash. "This is dumb," she said to Nate as they stood in the empty commercial kitchen. Ben had snuck off to who-knows-where to read the full autopsy report Nate had emailed him. "LaCena's dead," she said. "Why don't we take it as a win and get the hell out of here?"

Nate swallowed a mouthful of sandwich he'd just made from about seventy-five dollars' worth of meats. "Because we're the good guys." He motioned to his hair, apparently forgetting the pilfered sandwich in his hand. "The ones with the white hats. We save the day."

Six's laugh sounded much more bitter than she'd intended. "Nothing good will come of this. Parker's already pissed, and the longer we stay in the cold, the worse the fallout."

Before Nate could answer—although the hard line of his jaw seemed to indicate he had no reply handy—his phone buzzed. The hardness left his face, replaced by surprise and maybe a touch of something else—something Six couldn't quite put a finger on. "It's H," he said. His eyes scanned the message, which he then showed to Six. "She found the neurotoxin."

"What?" Six yelped. "How?"

Nate shrugged. "No idea. But I trust her when she says she found it."

Six wasn't so sure. H worked for Parker. For all they knew, he was playing with them, dangling the truth just out of reach, like he had with the poisoned Scotch. Six hated being kept on a string. "So what was it?"

"It definitely wasn't a poison that killed LaCena."

"No, it wasn't." Detective Bonewell appeared in the doorway, his face stony. "But you already knew that, didn't you, Ms. Barber?"

Chapter 18

✼

"Care to explain the traces of neurotoxin on your purse?" Detective Bonewell asked, a sneer distorting his bulldog-like visage.

Six glanced at Nate, and then at the detective. "I … ah …."

"Detective," Nate said, positioning Hannah behind his broad back. "Can I have a word?"

Bonewell nodded, allowing Nate to lead him to the doorway of the kitchen. "What I'm about to tell you must stay inside this room. Do you agree?" Nate asked quietly. When the detective nodded again, Nate smiled. He had the man in his pocket. It was like being back home, conning the locals out of their hard-earned dollars. "My being here isn't a coincidence."

"Is that so?"

"The FBI has been keeping close tabs on the victim for quite some time. Tonight," he paused, lowering his voice, "we had our best informants working surveillance."

The detective's brow knitted. "Her?"

"She's damned good." For once Nate was telling the truth. Six was a hell of an agent. *Not as good as me though*, he thought with a grin. "I'm telling you this in the strictest confidence. If anyone," he paused for effect, after all, you had to keep the mark interested, "finds out Ms. Barber is an informant …."

Bonewell chewed on his bottom lip as if debating whether or not to buy Nate's story. Nate gave him his most sincere smile. "Ms. Barber was trying to render aid, Detective. Nothing more. The neurotoxin must've rubbed off on her hands and then later her purse when she started CPR."

"According to my ME," the detective replied, "tetrodotoxin can't be 'rubbed' off, as you put it. She had to come into direct contact with it."

Nate's phone buzzed to life. He glanced down at the screen, noting the incoming message: *URGENT*. "I'm sorry, Detective, but I have to take this."

"Of course. We can continue this discussion at another time. For now, I'll re-interview the staff. Something's not quite right there, but for the life of me, I can't put my finger on it."

"I'll catch up with you in a bit," Nate said, his attention focused solely on the words H had typed on the screen. *Parker is on his way.*

Things were about to get a whole lot more interesting.

And possibly a whole lot worse.

~~~

BEN'S MIND WASN'T ON Parker as he scanned the dining

room where LaCena had flat-lined. No, his attention was focused on the suspects who filled the room. Any one of them could be a killer. Or more to the point, the Reaper. Since no one had ever seen the assassin's face, Ben scrutinized each suspect. Assassins, by trade, were careful and concise. It paid to be organized and more important, watchful. One never knew when an assassination could go to hell.

Only those who attended to every detail and responded accordingly survived this life. Sometimes Ben hated it—hated taking orders and hated distancing himself from everyone, even those he relied on to keep him alive. Six floated through his mind. While the two assassins worked as one during a mission, they rarely shared anything of a personal nature. It was for the best. 'Personal' got assassins killed. Ben wasn't about to make that mistake.

One of the diners caught Ben's eye. The man stood with his hands at his sides, but he was far from relaxed. The tendons in his forearms were bunched, as if he was ready to strike. Ben moved closer. Dressed much like the other diners in a sports coat and slacks, the man appeared to be just one of the hungry lot. But his eyes told a different story. They never stopped moving, scanning the crowd. He was either looking for someone intently or he was a killer. Ben suspected the latter.

"Some night, huh?" Ben said to the man, his eyes searching for any sign of a weapon. Finding none, he took a step closer. The man backed up a step, his eyes dancing over Ben to scan the crowd behind him.

"What?"

Damn. The man wasn't a killer. He was a drug addict with a stash and a strong mistrust of the men and women in blue surrounding him. Ben moved on, once again searching the crowd. A curvy woman by the doors looked vaguely familiar. Not her blonde hair or her cute, perky features, but something about the way she held her space. The way she motioned with the back of her hand when responding to whatever the policeman asked. For some inexplicable reason, out of the sixty or so diners, this woman stood out like a beacon on a dark and stormy night.

Ben strolled close enough to eavesdrop. "Mr. LeCena comes in every week at the same time," she was saying.

The cop raised an eyebrow. "You kept track?"

She sighed. "It's my job. A good maître d' knows her customers."

Recognition clicked into place: this was the woman who'd seated Six and Ben earlier. The one with the flirty smile. But something else about her still niggled at him, like a splinter just below the skin. "Excuse me," he said in his best 'just the facts' tone. "Was there anything unusual about your interaction with the victim tonight? Did he say anything or ask for anything different?"

The cop glared at Ben.

Oops. He'd forgot his role as typical diner. Wincing, he added, "I'm a true-crime buff."

That seemed to satisfy the cop, who was likely tired of taking witness statements. He nodded and closed his notebook. "I'm done here anyway." With that, he turned and left.

The hostess turned to face Ben, her eyes alight. "I love true crime too. I can't get enough of murder and mayhem."

A shiver ran down Ben's neck. He chalked it up to the air conditioning vent above his head. "Be that as it may, it must've come as quite a shock when one of your own customers dropped dead in front of you."

"Shock doesn't begin to cover it." She lowered her voice enough so Ben had to move closer to hear her. "But I'm not surprised someone wanted him dead."

"Is that so?"

Her head bobbed up and down, sending her hair dancing around her face. "He wasn't a nice man."

As far as understatements went, hers ranked in the top three of all time. "Oh? Did you know him well?" Was it possible that his murder was personal and had nothing to do with politics? Ben didn't think so, but providing Bonewell with enough reasonable doubt might deliver Six from his clutches.

"Not well. Enough to say a polite hello when he arrived," the woman replied. "Tonight though," she paused, running her tongue seductively across her teeth, "I could tell something was off. For one thing, he was late, and when he came in, he had his phone in his hand."

"That wasn't normal?"

Her eyes darted to the front door as if weighing how much she should tell a complete stranger. The internal debate didn't last long. It never did—a fact Ben relied on. People loved to gossip. To be the conveyors of scandalous news. "What wasn't normal was, he wasn't on it. It rang while I showed him to his table, but he didn't answer. And now he's dead …."

Ben cocked his head, unsure of her point.

"Maybe if he'd answered, that woman," she motioned to the kitchen where Six hid from the curious stares of the other diners, "wouldn't have killed him." Her hand flew to her mouth as if she'd just recalled Ben's relationship to Six. "I'm so sorry ... I didn't mean ...."

"It's okay," he said, his gaze on the woman's hand.

Or rather, the small inch-long tattoo running down her thumb.

A tattoo of a scythe.

Chapter 19

~~~

Parker Langdon had spent much of his life rising through the ranks of the CIA based solely on his pedigree. Unlike many of his colleagues with affluent backgrounds, Parker actually cared about his position as Director of OPS. Not only did he appreciate the prestige it provided and the hint of danger that drove women wild, but he was also convinced his work made the world a better place. Parker believed in the red, white, and blue of the flag that flew above the nation's capital.

He also believed in the power of green.

That money could solve any problem.

His point had been proven time and again. But when money did fail—a rare occurrence—force did the trick. It helped that Parker had over a hundred men and women at his disposal, ready and willing to act on his orders.

At this very moment, his most valued assassins were ignoring those orders. That alone drove him crazy. Add in that his best analyst was working behind his back to help one of the rogue agents and Parker had had more than enough. Benjamin Miller and his colleagues needed to know who was in charge. And so he had decided to handle this matter personally. He fingered the Smith & Wesson .380 hidden in the holster under his jacket.

~~~

Ben stood in front of Six, casually leaning against the kitchen counter, looking as if he didn't have a care in the world. She took in his relaxed posture and the hairs on the back of her neck rose. Ben didn't do casual. His pose was intended to induce a calming atmosphere for those under his command. He ran his thumb over the crystal glass next to him. "I've seen the hostess before. Well, not her, but the tattoo on her hand. I've seen it somewhere—"

"A naked somewhere?" Six joked, trying to hide the jealousy rising inside her. The thought of Ben and the hostess together disgusted her. He could do so much better than a bottled blonde. She frowned, catching the reflection of her own bottled blonde hair in the shiny surface of the industrial refrigerator.

Ben seemed to consider her words.

Moments ticked by.

"Damn it, did you sleep with her or not?"

He laughed. "Not that I know of. But you know how it is ... a lonely assassin on the road ...."

"Shut up," she said with a grin.

Ben frowned, all humor leaving his face. "Paris. Last year."

"What?" As far as Six knew Ben hadn't been in Paris since he'd divorced the fashion model. Unless he was keeping secrets from her. A real possibility, considering it had taken her a year to learn his birth date. She'd had to sneak into the HR files to find it. She still remembered the look on his face when she handed him a birthday card with a puppy on the cover, wishing him a 'very barky birfday.'

Ben's next words snapped Six back to the problem at hand. "The Ito killings."

The world shifted beneath her feet at his mention of the brutal murder of two Japanese businessmen the year before. Each man had been stripped to his underwear and then executed in an expensive hotel suite overlooking the Eiffel Tower. "You were there?"

Ben shook his head. "No. But Paul," he said, referring to OPS' second in command, "sent me the surveillance video."

"Why?"

"He suspected there was more to the murders than a simple robbery."

When he didn't elaborate, she prompted, "And?"

"I can't quite put my finger on it, but there is something similar about these two scenarios." Ben started to pace the kitchen, mindlessly rubbing his chin. Six smiled. Mannerisms got assassins killed because it made their behavior predictable, so Ben prided himself on not having any. Six knew better. When he rubbed his chin, it meant a plan was brewing inside his head—a plan that usually ended with Six leaping off a building or dodging guerilla fighters in one hundred and twenty degree weather. Ben stopped in his tracks. "Where's Taylor?"

Frowning at the abrupt change in subject, Six motioned to the dining room and said with a snarky tone and an eye roll for added sarcastic emphasis, "Not that it's my day to watch him, but he got an urgent text and left the kitchen about ten minutes ago. I haven't seen him since."

Ben shot her his own exaggerated eye roll. "We need that surveillance footage. If we can connect the hostess to the Ito killings, we just might've unveiled the Reaper."

"The hostess? No way."

"Why not?"

She swallowed, reluctant to utter the words on her lips. "Because … it's just …."

He laughed. "She's a she, and poor little Six likes to be the only murderous lady in the club." She took a menacing step toward him. He held up his hands. "Take it easy. I'm kidding." Pausing, he gave her a broad wink. "No one thinks of you as a lady."

Chapter 20

〜

BEN RUBBED HIS ARM, wincing as his fingers touched the Six-fist-shaped bruise. Maybe he should've kept the 'lady' comment to himself. He glanced over at his partner, who still looked ready to kill him, and grinned. The pain was worth it. "Can H get the video?" Ben asked Taylor, who leaned against the wall a few feet away, his long legs crossed at the ankles.

"She should have it in a minute." As Nate spoke, his phone buzzed. He gazed at the message, then looked back up at Ben. "The video's been flagged."

"Damn."

"So what now?" Six asked, frustration evident in her tone.

"I can call—"

Nate interrupted. "I said the video is flagged, not that H couldn't get it. She just has to be careful not to set off an alert."

Ben wondered why anyone at the agency would flag a surveillance video from a supposed robbery gone bad. Fuller had sent him the video six months ago, and it hadn't been flagged at that time. Yet one more secret at an agency full of them. "How long?"

"Ten minutes max."

Ben nodded. "Six, why don't you keep an eye on our hostess while we wait?"

"Your wish is my command," she mumbled under her breath, loud enough for Ben to overhear. He smiled, rubbing his bruised arm once again.

~

Six watched the hostess interact with her co-workers and the occasional cop. She tried to see the woman as an infamous murderer, but she just wasn't buying it. For one, the hostess liked to flirt—useful for someone in the restaurant industry but not so great for an assassin. Anything that got you noticed could get you killed. From personal experience, Six knew the dangers of attracting attention to oneself. Tonight's debacle was a case in point.

Moving closer to her target, she decided to resolve this matter once and for all.

Before Six could reach the woman, Ben appeared behind her. She recognized the faint footfalls of his highly polished shoes. "I wasn't going to touch her," she lied.

"I believe you," he said, but they both knew he didn't. "Video's here."

She glanced at the hostess then back at Ben. "Okay."

"Good girl."

"I will hurt you," Six said in a growl.

His eyes lit up, turning molten green. He shot her a grin

devastating enough to set her panties on fire. "Is that a promise?"

She stared into his eyes. Seconds passed as the noise in the room, as well as the danger they faced, faded. It was just the two of them. Ben leaned in. She moved to meet him halfway.

A crash sounded from the front of the room as a waiter dropped a tray of drinks.

The two assassins leapt apart.

~

NATE GLANCED FROM ONE assassin to the other. Something had happened between them. Hannah's face was flushed, and Miller didn't look much better. "Did I miss something?"

Ben shook his head. "Play the video."

He complied. The footage was of the hotel's lobby. Men and women in business suits passed by the camera, unaware of the surveillance. One of the security personnel filled the screen long enough to adjust or refocus the camera. The assassins stared at the screen, waiting.

"Pause it. Rewind. Now stop," Ben said. When Nate did as he asked, Ben pointed to the upper left hand corner of the screen. "Play it back. Slowly." A few seconds later, he said, "See that?" A person's arm flickered on the video for the briefest of moments and then it was gone. "See the tattoo," he said, his voice vibrating with excitement. "It's the same tattoo. Same place on her hand."

"You can't be serious," Nate said. "What do you have, eagle eyes?"

Ben laughed. "Not quite. I've watched this video at least a hundred times."

"Why?" Six asked, a crease between her brows. "I don't get it. What is it about these murders that makes you so suspicious?"

Ben ran his hand through his hair, not quite sure how to explain it. "These murders … they were all about the distraction. The Reaper killed the victims while fifty or so French cops swarmed the floors below after someone tripped an alarm in the hotel's safe, leaving plenty of time to get away with no one the wiser."

"So?" Nate said with a shrug. "We do the same thing all the time." It was straight out of the assassin's handbook, if there had been a handbook. Distract the target, and then take them out.

"True," Six said, "but we create the distraction. We don't use one that's already in place." She smiled as if she finally understood Ben's point. "Think about it. LeCena's murderer knew about us, used us as the distraction. The same way the robbery was used in France. It has to be the Reaper. Which means, since she was there—"

"The hostess is our killer." Nate tapped the screen, enlarging the scythe tattoo running down the mysterious appendage. "And we have her on tape."

Chapter 21

✺

"REPLAY THE RESTAURANT SURVEILLANCE," Ben told Nate. Nate cued up the video, and once again, the three assassins stared at the three-inch phone screen. "Go back," Ben said when the video showed Six approaching LeCena's table for the first time. "I want to see what happened when LeCena arrived."

The video slowly rewound, frame by frame, until LeCena disappeared from the screen. The hostess stood at her station. Waiting, perhaps? "Okay, play it," Ben said. Again all six assassins' eyes locked on the screen. LeCena and his bodyguards walked into the restaurant as if they owned it, pushing through the crowd of people waiting for their tables. When they arrived at the hostess station, the hostess smiled vaguely, motioning to his table. Wait staff bustled around, readying it for his arrival. He said something that annoyed her, if the set of her jaw was any indication.

The whole encounter took less than a minute and looked completely innocent.

Until LeCena dropped his cell phone.

The hostess grabbed it mid-air, switched it to her other hand, and then handed it back to him with another vague smile.

All three assassins looked up and grinned, their smiles anything but ambiguous.

~~~

Six couldn't believe their luck. They'd uncovered an infamous, formerly faceless killer. The CIA, FBI, NSA, and any other acronym one could think of had been after the Reaper for years. Without so much as a fingerprint left at any of the scenes. Not a trace of hair. Nothing. No one had ever suspected a female. They never did. It was one of the reasons Six was so effective.

But somehow, tonight, the Reaper had slipped up.

Right. Six had long ago stopped believing in luck. In fate.

So why now? Why tonight? She said as much to her fellow assassins, both of whom looked equally uncomfortable with the question. None of them had a good answer. But that didn't stop them from getting their job done. Ben motioned for Nate to flank his right, and Six his left. The idea was to surround the killer before she had a chance to hurt anyone or escape.

Six grabbed Ben's forearm as he stepped forward. He glanced down at her hand and then up at her face. "Be careful," she whispered in warning.

He nodded.

She let him go, and the three assassins moved out of

the kitchen as one. They had a simple goal: capture a killer with little collateral damage. Their own safety didn't matter, but the restaurant was filled with potential hostages. If the hostess felt trapped, there was no telling how she would react. Things could get bloody in a hurry.

Ben stopped dead in his tracks outside the kitchen doors. Six nearly ran into his broad back. "What is it?" she asked, his body humming with tension.

"Fuck," he said, voice grim. "Want the bad or even worse news?"

"Bad, please."

Ben turned to her, leaning down so as not to be overheard. "You probably won't be shooting anyone anytime soon. Our killer has vanished."

"No." Six peeked around his shoulder. Sure enough, the hostess had disappeared. And worse yet, so had the customers. Detective Bonewell stood by the front door, waving to the last of the disappearing diners. "What the hell?" she asked.

"Detective," Nate pushed from behind Ben and Six, "what's going on?"

The detective looked from the front door to the trio of assassins. "One of these upstanding citizens called the governor. He called the chief, and the chief called my boss." He motioned with the phone in his hand. "And he called me, saying in no uncertain terms that I was to release each and every person, apologizing to them individually for the trouble."

"What about the employees?" Nate yelled. "Are they gone too?"

Bonewell nodded.

"Shit," Ben hissed.

Nate grabbed the lapel of Bonewell's jacket. "The hostess. Tell me you have an address for her."

"Hey, watch it." The detective shoved Nate away. For a moment, Six worried Nate would lose control, but he held himself in check, merely biting out, "Give me her address."

Bonewell's face paled. "Is she ... did she kill—"

"The address. Now."

He flipped open his notebook, running his finger down page after page. When Nate started tapping his foot, the detective scrolled faster, finally saying, "Aha!"

Nate snatched the notebook out of the detective's hand and reached for the cell phone in his pocket. He quickly typed in the address and sent it off to H. Thirty seconds later, his phone buzzed. He glanced down at the message as Six held her breath. When Nate looked up, the anger burning in his eyes said it all.

"No such address," Ben said.

Nate nodded. "What now?"

"Now, you go home," Parker Langdon ordered from the inside of the doorway.

Chapter 22

~~

L OOKS LIKE THE PARTY'S over," Ben said, motioning to his fellow assassins. "You two wait here."

"No," Six said at the same time as Nate. "We are all in this," she paused, "together."

"Have it your way," Ben smiled grimly, "but don't blame me when we're all holding 'will kill for food' signs on the street corner."

Flanking Ben on each side, the assassins approached Parker, slowly, as if expecting him to strike. Parker's cold smile added to Six's trepidation. They'd disobeyed a direct order, and not only that, the man they were supposed to kill—or maybe not kill—had died at the hands of another. This sort of screw-up cost jobs, if not lives.

Then there was the whole 'killer on the loose' issue.

If they survived the next ten minutes with their jobs, she'd count them lucky.

~~

"Status," Parker snapped when the trio arrived at his side. Ben, who faced far more dangerous men on a daily basis, didn't bother to hid his disgust. If Parker wanted to throw his weight around, Ben would let him. As long as that weight stayed firmly directed at him, and not his fellow assassins. After all, they had not been the ones who had let a nice—very nice, in fact—set of legs distract them from their mission. If Ben been paying more attention to the matter at hand than Six's shapely calves and thighs, LaCena would still be dead, but by the right hand.

And the hostess wouldn't be in the wind.

He knew what would be keeping him up tonight—second-guessing. Not that he let his regrets show. Not now. "We're eighty percent sure we know who was responsible for LeCena's murder," Ben said. "Give us another hour, and we will wrap this up in a nice neat bow." Since the hostess had disappeared with a fake forwarding address, an hour seemed like a stretch, but what Parker didn't know wouldn't kill him—or earn Ben a bullet in the cranium.

Parker frowned, as if he expected a far different answer. "Your bow is already tied. I want the three of you out of here. This minute."

"But—"

Parker glanced at his watch. "Tomorrow, 0800, in my office for a debrief." With those words hanging in the air, he gave Ben a curt nod and left the restaurant. Staring at his retreating back, Ben said to the other assassins, "That was fun."

Six grinned, but the humor didn't reach her eyes. Ben tilted his head. He'd seen that look in her eyes a few times before, right before things went to hell. "What's up? What are you thinking?"

Six stared at the detective, who stood about ten feet away, ignoring the assassins as he read something on his phone; then she ran her tongue across her bottom teeth.

Ben swallowed hard, his blood rushing south.

"Don't you find the timing of Parker's 'visit' a little strange? Not to mention his coming down here in the first place." She crossed her arms over her chest. "You know him. When was the last time you saw him in the field, getting his manicured hands dirty?"

"She's right," Nate said. "We're still missing something." He winced. "Besides a killer hostess."

His gaze steady on Six, Ben said, "We have our orders. We leave it and her alone."

"But—"

"No," he said, not liking it any better than his fellow assassins. Letting a hired killer just walk away made his gut hurt. But they had their orders, and Ben and his team would obey them. Nate looked ready to argue, but Six waved him off. "It won't do any good. Ben won't disobey a direct order. He's too stubborn."

"Hey," Ben began. "This isn't about me. Or even us."

"Be that as it may," she paused, licking her lips, "I, for one, would love to get out of these heels and into a nice, soft bed, so let's do as Parker said, call it 'mission incomplete' and head out."

Ben swallowed hard at the image that popped into his head when Six said the words 'nice, soft bed.' He quickly shook off his fantasy. "Taylor," he said to Nate as he stuck out his hand, "thanks, man. We owe you."

Nate glanced down at Ben's outstretched hand,

frowning. Ben extended his reach, understanding Nate's hesitation. None of the assassins felt right about leaving a killer on the loose, but Ben knew better than to press Parker right now. Tomorrow he'd quietly contact his sources, see if anyone knew anything about LeCena's hit or the hostess. He would find her and end this. Just not tonight.

"Fine," Nate said, taking Ben's hand, "but I have a bad feeling about this."

Ben nodded. "You're not the only one."

Chapter 23

THE DRIVE BACK TO his apartment didn't lessen the feeling of impending doom in Nate's gut one bit. In fact, it increased it tenfold. *I should've never left Miller and Hannah at the restaurant*, he thought, his hand tightening on the gear shift. But Miller had given him his walking papers, ending Nate's 'official' involvement. A premonition flashed through Nate's mind, a Taylor family curse some called *The Sight*. In the jumbled vision, he watched as Ben and Six fired their weapons, but they were too late. He saw red—blood red—and then only blackness. What it meant, Nate had no idea, but he had to warn his fellow assassins.

He pulled his car over, dialing Ben's number on his mobile, but his call went straight to voicemail. He tried Six. She answered, sounding annoyed. "Nate," she said, "what's up?"

"I …" Nate wasn't sure what to say or how to explain the

blood-soaked vision. "You and Miller need to watch your six," he said, using the military term for ass. "Something's off."

There was silence on the other end. Finally Hannah said, "Will do. But don't worry. As soon as we find the good detective, we are leaving. We'll talk in the morning before our 'debrief.' "

Nate agreed and hung up, feeling a little better. He stared at his phone.

Maybe I should text H, see if she wants to meet up, in person for once, he thought but quickly dismissed it. Things were good. Best to leave their relationship as it was. Better to be safe than sorry. After all, he'd already fucked up once when he said 'I do' to his ex-wife.

The wisps of doom drifted through him again, but he shook the feeling off. His mind was playing tricks on him, that was all. Miller and Hannah were fine.

Nobody was going to die tonight.

Nate barely had time to recognize the irony of this thought half an hour later as two bullets slammed into his chest and his vision faded to black.

Chapter 24

“THAT WAS WEIRD,” Six said to Ben, holding out her cell phone when Ben finished the call he was on. “Nate called.”

Ben barely glanced up, clearly distracted by the news he’d just heard. It was probably one of his girlfriends, Six thought, hating the frisson of jealousy that claimed her. *He’s free to sleep with whomever he wants*, she reminded herself. Again. “Yeah?” Ben said when she didn’t add to her original comment. “What did he want?”

She shrugged. “I don’t know. He warned us to watch our backs. That was it.”

“Huh.”

“What’s that supposed to mean?”

He finally gave her his full attention. “We might have a problem.”

Jealousy quickly changed to fear. She hadn’t detected this tone in his voice for a long time. It was his ‘we’re fucked' tone. She swallowed hard. They'd survived a whole lot of horrible things before, and she hoped they would continue to do so. "Let's hear it," she said.

Ben rubbed his chin. "That was the chief of police," he said, waving his cell in the air. "He never ordered the diners to be released."

"Why would Bonewell lie?"

He shrugged. "Maybe he didn't. Someone else could've called his captain with the order."

"The hostess?"

Again he shrugged.

"She could've bribed Bonewell to lie." Her head tilted to one side. "He doesn't strike me as all that upright and moral."

"We should go ask the good detective."

Cracking her knuckles in anticipation, she grinned. "I'm looking forward to it."

He laughed. "I saw him in the kitchen about ten minutes ago." He motioned her forward. "After you."

"Ten bucks says I can make him cry."

"You're on," he said, already pulling the money from his wallet.

All her amusement vanished as she walked through the kitchen toward the exit door, which was slightly ajar. The coopery scent of fresh blood tickled her senses, a smell she'd thought she'd eventually grow accustomed to. She never had—not even close. Her stomach roiled, and she choked back the bile. She would rather swallow her tongue than show Ben a hint of weakness.

"Six," he said quietly.

She nodded, pulling her weapon from the holster on her thigh. Without another word, the two assassins maneuvered to each side of the exit door. Ben held his gun aloft. Using it to push the door wide, he went in low. Six followed, keeping her arms just over Ben's broad shoulder.

The assassins spilled into the alleyway just outside the kitchen. The odor of blood and decaying food nearly overpowered Six. She took a shallow breath through her mouth, adjusting to the stench.

"Clear," Ben said, after sweeping the alley with his gun for danger.

Six didn't respond, her gaze too intent on the lone foot sticking out of the Dumpster. Ben winced, pulling himself up for a better look at the body dumped like yesterday's garbage. When he recognized the bloated, badly beaten face, he said, "Call Taylor."

Six did as he asked.

The phone rang and rang.

The two assassins glanced at each other and ran for Ben's car, parked in the lot.

Chapter 25

～～

NATE WHISTLED TUNELESSLY AS he approached his apartment complex. The street was dark, and only an occasional car passed by. He appreciated the quiet after a long night. A bark drew his attention. No doubt Archie, his three-legged beast, had heard his car approach from a mile away. *So much for the quiet*, he thought as Archie's barks grew louder.

The sound sharpened his focus in the blackness surrounding him.

Unconsciously, his right hand moved to the gun holstered at his side.

His phone buzzed. Nate pulled it from his pocket and quickly glanced at the message from H. It was one word: *Tetrodotoxin*. His brow furrowed. Where had he heard that word before? Then it came to him, with terrifying clarity.

Ms. Barber was trying to render aid, Nate had said to

Detective Bonewell. *Nothing more. The neurotoxin must've rubbed off when she started CPR.*

The detective had responded, *Tetrodotoxin can't be 'rubbed' off, as you put it.*

Tetrodotoxin. How had the detective known the name of the neurotoxin? The medical examiner didn't. The other cops didn't. Hell, even H didn't have that information yet. Which could only mean one thing ….

"That son of a bitch," Nate muttered, spinning around to head back to his car. He hoped he wasn't too late.

But he was.

About two seconds too late.

The first slug caught Nate in the upper chest, sending him reeling. The second bullet wasn't as high, hitting him dead center in the chest. The pain barely registered as he managed to yank his weapon free. Blood … so much blood made holding onto the gun long enough to fire nearly impossible. He fumbled with the gun, sending it bouncing to the concrete next to him. He tried to reach for it, but the effort sapped his remaining strength. Grayness seeped into his vision, quickly going to black as two more shots filled the once peaceful night.

Then everything went black.

~

AS THE BULLETS RIPPED into Nate's body, Ben's car screeched to a stop in front of him. The assassins inside watched in horror and disbelief as Nate fell backward onto the concrete, a puddle of blood already filling the sidewalk. The Reaper spun toward the vehicle, weapon at the ready.

First out of the car, Six drew her own gun.

She took aim and fired.

Ben discharged his own weapon a second later.

Six's bullet struck the Reaper in the heart. While Ben's ripped through Detective Richard Bonewell's head.

—

Chapter 26

~~~~

Hours later, Ben walked Six to her apartment, stopping at her front door. Both assassins, Nate's blood drying on their clothing, were ready to call it a night. They'd spent the last three hours at the hospital as their fellow assassin clung to life. One of Bonewell's bullets had lodged less than an inch from his heart. The doctors weren't sure if he'd survive.

Ben shared their pessimism.

He'd seen men succumb to lesser wounds. Watched as the light was extinguished from their eyes and the breath rattled in their throats. *I need a new life*, he thought sadly, *one without treachery at every turn.*

One without blood and death.

He glanced at his partner, her face pale in the moonlight spilling from a nearby window. She looked … desperate. Ben knew the feeling well. They'd killed a bad man tonight and now would likely lose one of their own.

It was late.

They were beyond tired.

"I still can't believe it," Six whispered. "No wonder the Reaper had never been caught. As a detective, he could simply walk away with any evidence against him."

That explained LeCena's wiped cell phone data. Whoever hired Bonewell must've wanted their connection to LeCena severed—a clean break. No ties to them. "I'll give him this; he *was* a smart guy," Ben said.

She shook her head. "Then why make the mistake and go after Nate?"

"Guess we'll never really know." He rubbed his chin absentmindedly. "But I suspect he thought Nate was on to him. Maybe he let something slip?" He blew out a breath. "If Taylor survives, we'll ask him."

A tear glistened on Six's eyelid, but she blinked it away so quickly Ben wondered if he'd imagined it. "*When* he survives, Ben. Not if, but when," she said tightly.

"One thing's clear."

She gave him a sideways glance.

"Parker saved our lives tonight." He frowned, thinking back to the minutes when the trio had walked from the kitchen into an empty dining area. He was pretty sure Bonewell had been about to try and take all three of them out. Bad odds. Then Parker had arrived, turning bad odds to really bad odds. Bonewell must've changed his mind and decided to go after Nate one on one.

Besides, he probably figured that keeping Six alive as a murder suspect was a good backup plan. He had the evidence and Six's DNA. It would've been easy enough to frame her fully.

He thought about the hostess and her tattoo. Had she

really been responsible for the hit in Japan? She had been up to no good in her job at the restaurant, that was clear. Why else would she provide a false address? Perhaps she'd been working with the Reaper all along, providing the distractions he'd needed to complete his missions, and when Ben and Six had gotten close to figuring it out, the Reaper had killed her.

Six swallowed hard, drawing him from his thoughts. "It was a close call tonight."

He nodded, unsure where she was going with this.

"When I think of what might've happened … what *did* happen to Nate …." She closed her eyes. He fought an overwhelming desire to take her in his arms and make promises he could never, ever keep. Reaching out to touch her face, he stopped, his hand inches away.

Six gave him a small, sad grin. "See you tomorrow." She paused as if offering both a goodbye and an invitation for something else. When he didn't move a muscle, she lowered her gaze. "Partner."

"Right. Partner."

Without another word, she unlocked her door and disappeared inside.

Ben stood staring at her closed door for a long time.

If you're wondering about Ben and Six's growing attraction and want to know what happens next, check out *The Assassin's Heart* or fall in love with Nate Taylor and his family in *The Assassin's Kiss*, coming in August, 2016.

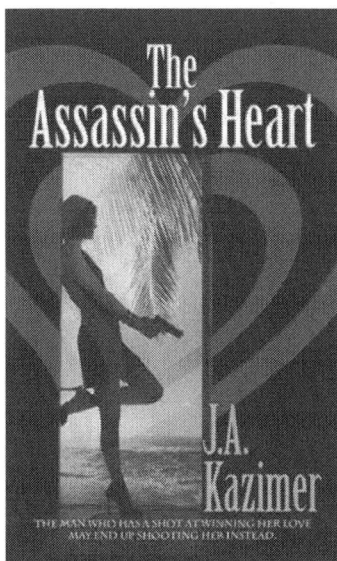

After "Six," a CIA assassin, mistakenly kills the wrong man, she vows never to take another life. Now her superiors, having concluded the killing was intentional, are targeting her. Six creates a new identity as an ad exec, but the past finally catches up with her at a company retreat in Hawaii, where her former partner Ben has tracked her down. Will Ben be her savior or her assassin?

Julia's estranged husband Nate won't sign the annulment papers. When she confronts him on his Florida houseboat, they are attacked by assassins. Unsure of the identity of their attackers or their intended target, Nate and Julia flee north. Unbeknownst to Julia, Nate is also an assassin, only for the government. As she learns more about her ex, she finds him harder than ever to resist.

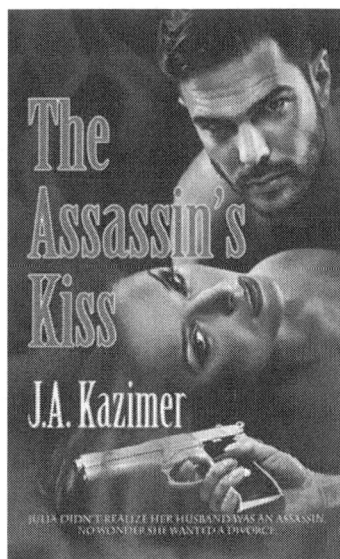

Cindy Miller

J.A. Kazimer lives in Denver, CO. When she isn't looking for the perfect place to hide the bodies, she spends her time surrounded by cats with attitude and a little puppy named Killer. Other hobbies include murdering houseplants. She has a master's degree in forensic psychology, which she promptly ignored and started writing novels. Prior to writing for a living, she spent a few years spilling drinks on people as a bartender and then another few years stalking people while working as a private investigator in the Denver area.

For more information, go to www.jakazimer.com.

Made in the USA
Lexington, KY
10 August 2016